Ty's One-man Band

Ty's One-man Band

by Mildred Pitts Walter

illustrations by Margot Tomes

FOUR WINDS PRESS   NEW YORK

LIBRARY OF CONGRESS CATALOGING IN PUBLICATION DATA

Walter, Mildred Pitts.
   Ty's one-man band.

   Summary: On a hot, humdrum day Ty meets a man who, using
a washboard, comb, spoons, and pail, fills that night with music.
   [1. Music — Fiction] I. Tomes, Margot. II. Title.
PZ7.W17125Ty   [E]   80-11224   ISBN 978-1-4814-5861-0

PUBLISHED BY FOUR WINDS PRESS
A DIVISION OF SCHOLASTIC MAGAZINES, INC., NEW YORK, N.Y.
TEXT COPYRIGHT © 1980 BY MILDRED PITTS WALTER
ILLUSTRATIONS COPYRIGHT © 1980 BY MARGOT TOMES
ALL RIGHTS RESERVED
PRINTED IN THE UNITED STATES OF AMERICA
LIBRARY OF CONGRESS CATALOG CARD NUMBER: 80-11224
1 2 3 4 5 84 83 82 81 80

For Adrienne, Keene, Mary and Sue

The sun rose aflame. It quickly dried the dew and baked the town. Another hot, humdrum day. Ty's mother was washing clothes, and his father was busy unloading feed for the chickens.

His sister was in the kitchen. Ty had nothing fun to do.

He knocked on his brother's door. "Jason," he asked, "want to come to the pond with me?"

"I'm busy," Jason said as he combed his hair. "Besides, it's too hot to go anywhere today."

Ty thought of the tall cool grass at the pond and decided to go there alone.

At the pond big trees sank their roots down deep and lifted their branches up, up, up toward the sky. The grass grew tall enough to hide a boy as big as Ty. He lay quiet, listening. Step-th-hump...
Ty pressed his ear to the ground. He heard it again: Step-th-hump step-th-hump, step-th-hump.

What could it be? Ty sat up. His heart beat wildly as he kept still, listening. Step-th-hump, step-th-hump. Not a slither, not a snake. And it was not a raccoon with her babies coming to fish in the pond. Raccoons grunt when hunting food and their babies make loud churr-rrr-rrr, churr-rrr-rrr's like a kitten's soft purr-rrr.

Step-th-hump; step-th-hump; step-th-hump, closer it came. Then Ty saw a man carrying a bundle. Ty had never seen anyone like this before. The man had only one leg. The other leg was nothing but a wooden peg.

The man walked down the path to the water's edge. He set his
bundle down. Then he bent his one knee, and with his peg leg
balanced in the air, he washed his face and hands in the pond. He
looks like a dancer, Ty thought.

The man took his time unfolding a red cloth. From the bundle he
took a tin cup, a tin plate, and a spoon. Then he took out cheese,

apples, and a big round loaf of bread. He nibbled the cheese to taste it. He smiled. Then he ate hungrily.

He washed his dishes in the pond and then did a surprising thing. He tossed his cup into the air and caught it. He tossed the plate and then the spoon. He's a juggler! Ty thought.

Again the man tossed the cup, plate, and spoon in the air one after the other, over and over and over very quickly and caught them all. Then he beat a rhythm with the spoon on the cup: tink-ki-tink-ki-ki-tink-ki-tink, tink-ki-tink-ki-ki-tink-ki-tink; and on the plate: tank-ka-tank-ka-ka-tank-ka-tank, tank-ka-tank-ka-ka-tank-ka-tank; and then on the cup and plate: tink-ki-tink-ki-tank, tink-ki-tink-ki-tank, tink-ki-tank-ka-tank, tink-ki-tank-ka-tank, tank-ka-tink-ka-tink-ka-tank, tank-ka-tink-ka-tink-ka-tank.

He's a drummer, too, Ty said to himself. Wonder if he's a circus man.

Ty still watched from the cool tall grass. The sun moved slowly up
to the center of the sky. Nothing stirred in the heat. Then there
was a low rumble like thunder afar. The train turned the bend:
woo-woo-woo-ee-ee-eee. Soon there was another thunderous roar

and a loud WOO-WOO-WOO-OO-EEE! Ty forgot the man and watched the train speed by, clackety-clackety-clackety-clack. The woo of the whistle and the clack of the wheels died away. Ty looked toward the pond for the man, but he was no longer there.

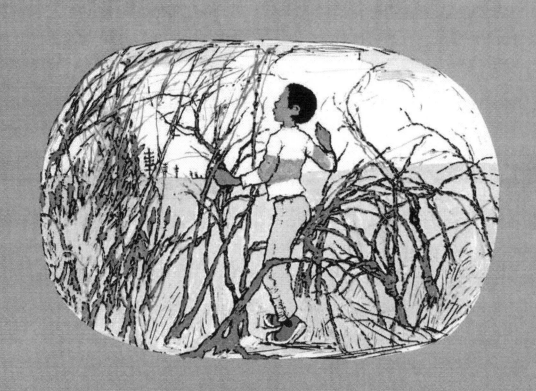

Ty peeped out of the tall grass. He looked to the left, then to the right and all around. How had the man disappeared so quickly, Ty wondered. Did he see me and hide? But where could he hide so quickly?

Slowly Ty moved out of the grass. Quietly he moved toward the trail. The crackle of twigs sounded like fireworks. He kept looking for the stranger. He looked in the bushes near the pond. Where had the man gone? Was he a disappearing magician, too? Ty tiptoed to the trail. He felt his heart beat thump, thump.

Just as he was almost to the trail—WHEE-EE-EET!
　　Ty screamed and froze.

The man jumped out of the grass and laughed and laughed. He laughed so hard that Ty began to laugh, too.

"Why are you tiptoeing around like that?" the man finally asked.

"I was looking for you. I thought you had disappeared," Ty said.

"Did you think I wasn't real? I didn't mean to scare you," the man said. "I only whistled for fun."

"Do it again," Ty said.

The man did it again. Then he whistled a tune and danced a step.

"Are you a circus man?" Ty asked.

"No. I'm not a circus man."

"Who are you?"

"My name is Andro. I'm a one-man band."

"What's a one-man band?"

"I'll show you. Go home and get a washboard and two wooden spoons, a tin pail and a comb. I'll come into town at sundown and make music for you and your friends."

Ty hurried home. A one-man band! Could he remember all those things to get? Wooden spoons, a tin pail, a washboard . . . there was something else. What had he forgotten? Ty tried to think. He scratched his head. A comb!

Wait'll I tell my friends, he thought. They'll come and hear the music, too.

At home Ty ran to Jason's room. "Can I use your comb at sundown for the one-man band?"

"For the what?" Jason asked.

Ty told Jason about the peg-legged man. "Come and bring your friends at sundown!" he said.

"Don't be silly. How can he make music with just those old things? My friends will laugh and yours will too if you try to tell them such a thing."

"But can I use your comb?"

"Yea, but combs are made for combing hair, not for making music."

Ty rushed to the kitchen. His sister was stirring corn bread. He told her about the man who was a band. "Can I use two wooden spoons at sundown?"

"Yea," his sister said, "if you promise to bring them back. These spoons have made a lot of good corn bread, but I never heard them make music." She laughed as Ty rushed off.

He found his mother in the yard, taking in clothes. He told her about Andro.

She shook her head. Then she said, "You may use my washboard at sundown. But that board is made for washing, not for making music."

His father was in the shed, putting corn in the pail to feed the chickens. "Of course, you may use the pail, son. But don't bet on hearing a one-man band. Pails are for hauling, not music."

Ty ran to tell his friends. No one believed there was such a thing as a one-man band. And how could a peg-legged man dance? How could he make music with a comb, washboard, or wooden spoons? Jason was right. All of Ty's friends laughed.

The sun turned into a glowing red ball. It sank lower and lower, but the town didn't cool. People fanned themselves on their porches. Ty's friends sat in their yards or sprawled on their steps. It was so hot they didn't even talk.

Ty sat on the corner under the street lamp. The comb, the pail, two wooden spoons, and the washboard were nearby. He waited. Would Andro come? And if he came, what kind of music would he make with Jason's comb, the old washboard, two wooden spoons, and a pail?

Twilight turned purple. Had Andro forgotten? Soon the street light came on. Ty's friends saw him still waiting.

"Hey, so you think the one-man band is coming, eh?" Ivan shouted.

"If he were coming, he'd be here by now," Nohl called.

"Washboard music? What's that?" Josh said. They all laughed.

"He will come. You'll see," Ty shouted at them.

Ty waited and waited. Could Andro find his way into town? Would he come? Ty waited some more. He was just about to pick up his things and go home.

Then in the darkness he heard a step-th-hump, step-th-hump, step-th-hump. He was coming! "Whee-ee-ttt! Whee-tt! Whee-ee-ttt!" Andro whistled.

Before Ty could speak, Andro turned upside down and walked toward Ty on his hands. "I'm here at your service," he said. He turned right side up and bowed low.

Ty just grinned.

Andro looked at all the things. He turned them about one by one. "These will make fine music," he said as he sat with his good leg folded under him.

He placed the spoons between his fingers and moved them very fast. Quack-quack-quacket-t-quack. The empty square filled with the sound of ducks. Then he made the sound of horses dancing slowly, clip-clop-clip-clop-clop. They danced faster, clipty-clop, clipty-clop, clipty-clop-clop. Faster still, cl-oo-pop, cl-oo-pop, cl-oo-pop-pop-pop-pop-pop. "Hi ho, Silver!" Andro shouted.

Ty clapped and clapped. Andro took a thin piece of tissue paper from his pocket. Carefully he folded the paper over the comb. Before Ty could ask what that was all about, Andro was making music.

Ty sang along when Andro played.
The music drifted through the empty streets,
around quiet corners. One by one people began
to leave their porches. They pressed in closer and

clapped their hands and tapped their feet as Andro played and
danced to his own music. His peg leg went tap-tap-ti-ti-tappity-
tap, tappity-tap-tap-ti-ti-tap. He twirled, skipped, hopped, and
danced 'round and 'round in the spotlight of the street lamp.

Andro stopped dancing and began to make sounds on the washboard. As he passed his fingers over the board, Ty could hear water falling, rushing down a hill over rocks, then gurgling in a stream, and then trickling to a drip, like from a faucet. Best of all were sounds of a big freight train puffing slowly, then faster, faster, faster still, then passing by with the whistle far away.

"More!" Ivan shouted.

"More! More!" Josh and Nohl cried.

Andro sat down. Now he held the pail under his arm and with his fingers drummed: di-di-did-d-d-dum, did-di-d-d-dum, de-le-di-di-doo, de-le-di-di-doo, diddle-dum-dum-doo, diddle-dum-dum-doo.

"More! More! More!" the people shouted.

Andro set the pail down. With a spoon in his hand, he hit the pail, his wooden leg, and the other spoon. Di-de-le-dum, di-de-le-dum, de-di-la-di-ti-do, de-di-la-de-ti-do, chuck-chick-chu-dum, chuck-chick-chu-dum.

Boys and girls, mothers and fathers, even the babies clapped their hands. Some danced in the street. Whenever the music stopped, everybody shouted, "More!"

Andro let Ty take turns using the instruments. Ty's friends
wanted turns, too. Soon the four of them played together like a
one-man band. Everybody danced. Only Ty saw Andro slip away

back into the night.

Made in the USA
Lexington, KY
22 June 2016